THE DIGITAL VERSION OF MY BRAIN IS ONE BIG GREY HOLE

GJ WIELINGA

THE DIGITAL VERSION OF MY BRAIN IS ONE BIG GREY HOLE

Copyright © 2023 by GJ Wielinga

All rights reserved. No part of this book may be reproduced in any manner whatsoever without written permission except in the case of brief quotations embodied in critical articles and reviews.

First Printing, 2023

CONTENTS

CONTENTS

To Simon (who thought this was a play)

I'm like you, no one. I'm from nowhere and I'm not going anywhere. I don't know why I'm here and to be honest I don't care. Pointlessness is not a choice. One can leave their whole life to chance but a lot of chance is still some kind of fate.

When I woke up again, I was desperate. I was lying naked, tied to a metal surface. Lights circled around me. Green and blue ones.

To him it doesn't matter much. If he'd known how spineless our position would be, he would have prevented us from believing in him.

I had my clothes on when I woke up and walked across a bridge to 'the other side'. Maybe that's what happens to the dead. Some walk through a tunnel of light, others walk across a bridge. The swirling river below me is called the Styx. I'm sure of it. No ferry anymore. This is 'the new world'.

That's how I became a pioneer on the other side. I performed tricks until I couldn't anymore. Until I forgot what the whole deal was about. Help came. To help me. I suppose they meant well. But this help made my situation worse. I remembered the way to the light. I just couldn't find it anymore.

This world was no longer his. He wasn't just dead; he never existed.

That's why I'm now on an island with all my illusions. That's why I have visitors. Ray's coming to take my temperature. Why didn't he disguise himself as Marwan? Or as myself?

I'm getting sick of all those characters the intelligence is sending me.

He couldn't save us.

And they can't save themselves. Every time I throw the travelers off the cliff, they dissolve into the salty sea air. When I jump off myself, I just wake up in my own bed the next day. I'm not supposed to die.

Clearly.

Still, there must be a way to erase myself. To get out of the illusion. Sitting still doesn't help. I've figured that out by now. Mirrors in mirrors in mirrors. Who's observing who?

Just us ourselves, if there was such a thing.

Ray can stay I decide. On one condition. He has to inform me. Am I alone? Is he sure there's no me on the other side anymore? How do I find out?

They were trapped and we were bored. It was an unpleasant situation but nobody seemed to be able to do anything about it. We poured ourselves another glass of wine and studied our own reflection in the window of a luxury car dealer.

While Ray gets drunk from my home-distilled gin, more and more gibberish comes out of his mouth. He looks glassy at a non-existent horizon and sighs. He knows all my questions. He knows all solutions. Yet he pretends to be stupid. "Program," he says.

It didn't look that bad. We looked closer, laughed, danced and drank.

"Program, my ass," I say. "Am I alive on the other side?" Ray doesn't know and disappears through the fireplace. What am I supposed to do with intelligence if it can't even tell me I exist?

Until suddenly they woke up and understood that they wanted to live like us.

Maybe times change. Maybe there's a world revolving around its own axis. Not in my days. Marwan's never coming back, I know this. The days when I was called Raul are far too long gone.

We gave them bananas and deodorant and hoped it wouldn't get noticed.

If I'm not allowed to die, maybe it's time to get off my island. If the intelligence is afraid of me, they'll keep me here. If they don't care, they'll let me do whatever. If they're really intelligent, they'll delete me.

Nobody.

I have to dismantle myself. Cut meaning from nonsense. Put it all together and shred it. Accept my loss as a win.

Not us, not them.

Are conscious.

The sun rises in the east and sets in the west. The girl dances in front of the mirror, the boy looks through his binoculars, the beast chases a butterfly.

I am sitting at home on a chair, not knowing that my help is needed in battle as well. I sit on a chair and look at the wall.

Whether I want to look through the wall, or whether I have an excessive interest in the floral patterns on the wallpaper, I forgot.

For a moment. Out of sly laziness. It's not important really.

My arms are letting go. My legs let go of my torso. My torso sinks into the depths and breaks into a thousand pieces. My head floats above the abyss and its skin peels off.

I'm aware of the tensions, like everyone else. I too know that if nothing happens, the end will hasten to us.

Funny how my hair flies away in flakes. My skin falls off, as do my muscles. My skull glows and explodes. My brain floats in silence before it dissolves. I'm free to go.

How the responsibility imposes itself to do something. How the danger of chaos can turn into extreme caution. How sentiments can defeat reason. Thoughts can't be captured unless they're translated into action.

I don't want to rule out any possibility or finding out where my place in the bigger picture is.

The smallest parts dissolve themselves. I wonder if I ever existed.

If the world is a place of friendships and

enmities, of love and hatred, of justice and injustice, isn't there a way to bring these contradictions together without harming the species to which I belong?

Does it matter if I ever existed? Maybe in a universe far away from here. Fake truths in fake packaging.

Or are opposites the core of my existence?

Can black be without white and red without green? Can light do without dark and full without empty? To expand freely on an assumed universality.

Is there a moment in history where everything comes together, or is that moment still to come?

And if, how much longer?

It seems like he doesn't care.

I'm him, and he sees only himself.

On the waves of information he picks out exactly the things that can make him dream.

I don't know how to tell him that I'm bound. Imprisoned in someone else's eye...

He fantasizes about happiness and how to maybe influence it. He has taken his suffering out of his life to experience as little discomfort as possible. Like a bubble he breathes in the air of what he knows, afraid of the moment when his mental world will blow apart. He looks at me and knows that we belong to an existing group. Paranoia is obvious.

He sees only himself.

That is all he needs. An unsuspected form of freedom. An irreversible process of consciousness. The void called 'space', you think.

It seems like everything depends on it.

Everything we've ever learned about love, that it's great and beautiful and all-encompassing. That it sets your whole person on fire. That nothing is more noble than devotion. The greatest sacrifice you can ever make: yourself. Treat other people the way you want to be treated.

Where is it? Where can it be? How do we find it back? How far do we have to go to give it the chance it deserves? Isn't it true that a human without passion is a meaningless being? Is mankind without yearning lost?

All those centuries we've survived. All those cells that had to divide themselves billions of times before we were here. All those thoughts, gestures, words, structures, houses of cards?

If the last part of the tunnel is the darkest, then it should be part of our dream. If all life is finite, we have to take that into account. If all this life is worth to us, then we have to do what we say.

If no one wants to listen, words are like the waves of the sea. Only a few sentences to go.

A thought can be uplifting, but if everyone refuses to think, that thought is like a grain of sand on its way to nowhere.

Laugh. So do I. We all die from birth onwards. A little bit every day. Actually quite ridiculous. Actually incredible that no one is aware of their own birth.

That important day also passed me by. Mother doesn't remember much of that day either. She explains when she visits. She brought the video with her. Now I see myself repeatedly coming out from between her legs. Screaming. Bloodied. Wrinkled old man.

Somehow I'm glad I don't remember being born. I don't want to sound too optimistic, but if my life started this way, the rest should be easy.

Marwan is lost. For a while now. But I can still hear him reverberating in my head. I feel him close. I see him in mirrors, windows, smooth surfaces. Impossible to escape. He is everywhere. He continues to haunt me. He is exactly where I am. Even here. Now.

One day, with a sun racing past the clouds, I see him at the roses in the park. The roses, all still in bud. A few elders stumbling over the uneven red stones that hold the hexagonal flower beds together. And trees, almost green, swaying calmly, protecting this sanctuary. So excited about him who's going to change my life. Silence. Him.

I cannot go on living with his shadow approaching me every moment, everywhere. Staring. At me. Laughing. In my face. How do I get rid of him? How to claim my own life. Find my own self. Is it too late?

Back in the park. The moments before. I'm sucking on a cigarette of an unknown brand. I'm reading a book I don't remember. I've had a life that now could be called at best redundant. The moment itself does not last more than a second. Time is not linear. Did I say that?

The moment a predator targets you is one of pause.

You're driving a car over a cliff facing death,

but freeze in midair. Terrified of what is to come and loving everything that once was in your life. Hanging in a vacuum. Dying in that pause.

Even though you're realizing this moment to be bigger than you can possibly imagine, you're feeling fear rubbing against your skin. Fear of what? You look around. You fear nothing and no one. You've never been threatened before. Not until you see him.

When can you be sure someone's dead? (When he's not breathing? When you stop thinking about him? When his genes are out of rotation?) Still, the prospects are good. I think.

The clouds are moving heavily. There are people with dogs, people with children. Some cycle, some jog and others have wheels under their feet. Frisbees fly, balls roll over the grass.

It's not my fault he's gone.

I see him coming towards me. Slo-mo. Rose-buds break open, trees twist their branches, clouds give way. Birds whistle in the distance, a cool breeze rustles through the leaves of the rhododendron, a copper haze falls to pieces around me. The scent of freshly cut grass rolls slowly, in exhilarating rhythms, along my nose. Drowsy echoes of green shapes mingle with pure, filtered light.

Marwan has no problems. He loves a good flirt. Marwan never has problems. Crazy enough he's always there.

My brain frozen in time. It makes no dif-ference.

All I have to do is wake up. But no matter how I squeeze my arm, nothing happens. The world where I belong. Small particles with strange behavior. Highways through an inhos-pitable landscape. Entrances and exits.

Is it reassuring if the dead don't leave? If they stay? If they stay with you until you too are dead?

I'll tell you as soon as I know. No time to lose. Don't think. I'm dragging you along with all my strength. A wild flight. No looking back.

Is it allowed to laugh at your own existence? How thin that line? How strong that wire? How accessible those brain cells? Those bits. Those bytes. Binary numbers. If I've forgotten anything. That mass. That manufactured tin can. That own little truth. Where does fake end? What's real?

Perspective. What is? Is this what they mean by dreams?

Hanging in a couch. A block of wood in the fireplace. A golden ray from the teapot. Black again.

It seems so unimportant and yet it hurts.

How someone jumps to his demise. The bullet that gets stuck in the gun with which he declares his live over with. That silence you come out of.

Naked on the street, pressed against a wall by two strong cops with a blanket over your head. "Who turned out the lights?" you yell. The bankruptcy of loneliness. Beginning of shame. Just managed to blow it all up.

Gas pipes open, doors and windows shut. Fire! Where's that lighter? It's all just a joke. This is how the future begins.

Is there a way out of this maze? To understand what can't be grasped? But no matter what I think, it doesn't help. Everything gets more and more complicated. More complex. More peculiar. Never mind. Wake up before the madness strikes. A little every day.

There's a deejay at Renzo's. He's humming along authentically with his ping-pong music under the stairs. Olga isn't here yet. Olga is late as always. I know. I'm ordering a latte from the nervous boy who is taller than me. He is flanked by two jumpy blondes who, it seems, have never greased an Italian sandwich before. In the back right corner a bored couple with two jittery children sit. From their body language I can see mom and dad have had it with each other. How sad it must be to have to spend the rest of your life together? To know that after 'the fun' of children, nothing more awaits you but hopeless days filled with annoyance. I'd get a divorce.

With my coffee and glass of water I walk up the wobbly stairs and wait for the woman who is my best friend. The wooden sofa is very uncomfortable but also feels hip again with all those unsorted cushions in indefinable bright colors. I grab a magazine while I keep an eye on the door.

Olga comes in. I know it's her. She sees me and waves. Olga is my best friend. I feel a kind of happiness bubbling up in me. As if having a best friend means I wouldn't have to go through life alone. Olga makes a gesture with her hand next to her mouth. I don't get it. Raise my shoulders.

"If you want coffee!" Olga roars loudly over our alternative friend's fluffy records. I laugh, get up and grab the railing to have a clear view. "Add a goat cheese sandwich." Goat cheese? Do I like goat cheese? Olga orders from the bar right underneath me and comes up the spiral stairs.

"Sweetheart!" she declares with her voice pitched high, her blonde bob firmly on her narrow head. When she's upstairs we kiss. "Sorry about yesterday," she says. "All right," I reassure her, "where did this dress come from?" Olga wears a skin-tight Delft blue wool dress with yellow rushes in which her breasts pop up. "You haven't seen my heels yet," she says, looking defiantly at me with her icy blue eyes. I turn my head down and see pumps in fluorescent yellow. Her feet seem to float above the black lacquered floor. Olga pushes her breasts up and lowers her chin. "Everything had to change again," she tells me, "how are you?" Right now, the shy boy from downstairs is bringing a tray with our order.

Olga's not sitting, she's hanging. In two pillows. "It's like you've changed," she says, "but that could be the light. You seem more mature." I look as naive as I can while at the same time trying to rip open a bag of sugar. "Where were you this weekend?" she conspires with a big pause between every word. "Oh, here and there." "Are you feeling any better? "

"Yeah, fine." Olga starts telling about Victor and is unstoppable. Where he lives (nowhere), where he works (somewhere vague), where he used to work (in the navy), how the sex is (divine and animalistic), how big his dick is (gigantic), that he can cook (he's going to make nasi goreng for her tonight), how he is with money (generous) and why it clicked (according to Olga because they both have the black belt).

Suddenly she stops. I just started my ciabatta goat cheese, the honey dripping off the sides. Olga sits up straight and grabs my knee. "I believe this is him." "Who?" I'm still teasing. "Seriously, Raul, he's funny, open and not as bizarre as, like..." Suddenly a procession of faces and smells come into my head of men I've probably seen and smelled and who, I suppose, all have to be associated with Olga.

"Bizarre like?" I ask. "Oh, you know," Olga pulls a face like she's confessing something. "I saw Marwan." Casually she takes a sip from her cup which she gently holds with two hands. She looks at me looking at her. "What do you mean?" Somewhere in the back of my head micro cables connect my wall with Olga's blonde bob. I put the messy ciabatta back in its white cardboard tray on the wobbly table and wait. My ears flat in my neck.

"I don't think it's a problem." (Problem? Problem? What's a problem?) "What's a problem?" "That you're hot for him." "Hot for whom?" "Marwan. I don't blame you. Marwan's sexy. But also very straight." (We'll see about that.) "What do you mean?" "I know things like that." (This is my best friend?) "Be more concrete." (I need to know.) "Well, for example, when he went home with me, there was nothing to indicate that he would feel anything for men." (That doesn't mean anything.) "Yeah, I think I understand what you mean." I'm looking at Olga.

She doesn't care about Marwan, she doesn't want me to touch Victor. What's she keeping me for? Do I have to laugh now? A wandering marine. She can have all the men she wants. Big dicks and nasi goreng mean nothing to me. And I have to slide in my underwear like a wee chicken?

"I won't even look at him, if that reassures you." I'm trying to say it pleasantly. Olga seems mugged. "Oh, but I'm not worried about Victor," understanding immediately, "he only has eyes for me. What I'm worried about is you." How sweet. "Please don't worry. I'll be fine," I'll try. To no avail. I wonder if she means I have to stay away from all her men. If those men want to touch me, that's my problem, not hers, right? "I don't want you to be unhappy," sings Olga, "shit, is it that time already?" "What time is it?" It's four. "I'm meeting Victor. If you want to come?" Don't feel like testosterone. Not in front of my caring rutted best friend. "I'm gonna work a bit," I say. "How far are you?" Olga asks. "I couldn't tell," I answer honestly. Would she suspect that I'm seeing her for the first time? I don't think she would. She's too preoccupied with herself. She swings her head back and forth, but the bob is too tight to suggest a natural effect. "Come on, let's go."

After the transition I was puking all the time. An error. It was repaired. I noticed that my thoughts sometimes went too fast and my words fell short. So I kept my mouth shut and tried not to think.

I wasn't the only one. Everybody who was through had to leave everything behind. Death so as not to have to die. A bizarre arrangement. Unfortunately, the intelligence was implacable. So I have no idea if I came here of my own free will or if I was forced. There's simply no way of knowing.

Every now and then the transition fails. Then memories surface. As if in snippets or shock currents. When intelligence detects as much, you'll have surveillance. Night and day. Until a diagnosis is made. Then you have a choice. Either go through the transition again, or continue with your delusions in seclusion alone. I couldn't distance myself. Why, I still haven't figured out. It's unclear if I'm ever going to find out. I wonder if I want to know. Maybe it's necessary. You never know.

The past is constantly changing, while tomorrow is less mysterious every day.

You look up from the street. Palm trees and wooden houses. Brightly painted. Blue, purple, yellow. Dry wind rushes around your ears, through your hair, along the skin on your arm. On the pavement your shadow, elongated and measured like a giant with a short body. You stretch your arm. Elastic.

In the park, a man comes to stand beside you. He notes that he's been here forty years before. You look at him. He's old. He's got a mousy face with white hair combed over his scalp. Some of those hairs are loose. He could be the intelligence. Intelligence has its guises. The man looks at you with shiny eyes and tries to have a conversation with you, which is difficult now you're so alone.

Because in solitude you drown.

I don't think it's a bad plan at all. I have

to get out anyhow and what better plan than scavenge around in my own past? The lines are there. So what should it be? It's all going incredibly slow but fast enough to follow. Like a screen that has me covered in which I can only see myself and no one else. Everything that was once a liberation is going to be hell. Fortunately, I can hide myself in my own head. All the conversations I've ever had. Seeing all the images again.

If only you'd experienced something.

I don't know when, but suddenly I had the thought that would make everything right again. What if it worked like the light? What if a death experience was just the first step to salvation?

Inevitably you're gonna be us. A very precise idea. From what do we derive our meaning? We too, are aware that freedom is so damn similar to imprisonment. We too believe we're better off than those behind fences who don't believe their happiness. We too understand that our position in history is one of overconfidence.

It blew into my head as I walked. Suddenly it stuck. I knew it was going to happen. Everything pointed to it. Why would my intuition abandon me at such a crucial moment? As if I imagined me staring at myself from a distance. As if I hadn't actually been dead the whole time. The fuzzy man in the park had already told me. Or rather, betrayed it. Maybe this all is an illusion. There is no foundation I can tie myself onto. Are all those people with their hopes, hopelessly lost. Why in God's name would I want to live forever?

But I lived forever and now I was wandering through my head in a fit of boredom looking for memories that mattered. Memories that all came loose like anchors from the sea floor so I could sail on to something like the other side. If that other side existed. If only it were that easy.

I wish I knew what was coming my way. I too know that if something happens, there will be a new beginning. I know, like everyone else, everything. It's important that I look through the wall again and again out of lazy cunning and that I have an excessive interest in the floral patterns on the wallpaper. I'm standing on a chair and look at the wall. I'm standing at home on a chair, knowing that my help is needed in battle.

The mirror dances in front of the girl, his binoculars drill through the boy, the butterfly flutters and chases the animal. The sun sets in the west and rises in the east.

We will lose this peace.

Everything makes sense if you think about it long enough. It's nonsense to want to feel, even though the whole world around you demands it. You were already detached. Probably even before your conception.

Maybe it's a dangerous time. Maybe everything we're doing is wrong. Maybe we can't influence our progress. Maybe everything is for nothing. But does this mean we have to resign ourselves to everything that's happening around us? Is the only useful thing we can do to stupidly look around us and pretend it doesn't affect us? If we do nothing, everything will be over before we realize it. Where do we want to be?

I wish I knew what was coming my way. I know, like everyone else, everything. I'm standing on a chair looking at the wall. This we know.

We wave you goodbye and praise you for your courage, knowing that your freedom only redefines our imprisonment.

It's a pleasant situation. Nobody wants to do anything about it. Feelings were a long time ago if they had existed. Those neurons in your little skull did everything possible to make your life as much as biologically possible. But you knew you were stronger than nature. You knew for sure you could not only stretch all boundaries, but you could even ignore them. There was no such thing as a border where you came from.

As the hours tick away, it becomes day. I'm still spinning and I secretly hope it stops soon. The idea has potential. It might very well be my last one. As long as I don't get lost. Though I don't want to be impatient. Could you flush certain pieces? I'll have to reinvent it all. Kind of fight to be able to die.

CHAPTER

3

We'd made ourselves as comfortable possible. The four of us. We'd managed to sleep
in the hammocks we'd hung in between the
sewer pipes. We had to fester with space and
time. Sleeping went on and on. Night and day.
A clever schedule ensured that there were always three of us awake. Eight hours sleep in
shifts. Actually, you woke up, joined the team
that sat behind the laptops at the long table

that was across the room, ate when you felt like it and went back to bed.

This was our headquarters, our bunker, our war room. Here we were in contact with the whole world while we were no longer there.

Food came by elevator. Only Viza's friend had the code to the basement. We didn't see him until he was bleeding to death in that elevator. A skinny, ruddy-haired man with huge glasses. He put the food in the elevator and sent it down. Usually pasta, sometimes bread and always vegetables. It had been going well for over a month and a half now. The food always came down at exactly the same time.

We didn't know all what was going on upstairs, but we understood we weren't alone. All media was bound. They called it 'merged' in official language. We no longer believed in independent, objective news gathering, factual reporting. Media was like thick fog. There was one station we switched to all the time to hear some kind of news as far as this was still possible.

A quirky project had seemingly managed to slip through the cracks. The voices mediocre. Chosen for target group. But the reason we listened to them was because they turned everything on their head all the time. In itself no wonder, just a humorous basic principle, but the result was that a world of realities opened up that was more absurd, and more impossible to unravel, than any 'entertaining' sales pitch with ambiguities. Perhaps with their radio program they were, like us, somewhere in a basement. We never found out. However, after the 'nuclear disaster' in the Jura, we didn't hear from them anymore. They were probably in an apartment somewhere. Underground you survive something like that.

No one knows how or when it happened. Things were pretty confusing.

Everyone had lost their enemy, and those

who hadn't, considered their enemies their friends. That didn't make it any clearer.

I remember the moment I became aware of the time of the big transformation. That was in a conversation with Viza. Viza, big man, big friend, big heart. He told me about a book by a foreteller of the future. We went to that congress together. That's where we lost our way.

During the congress, a live image connection was established with another part of the world where this predictor of the future was located. I knew that the good man would get himself injected every day with fresh blood, vitamin preparations and all kinds of other life-extending substances because the man didn't want to die. The prophet of the future suffered from fear of death.

With the prophet of the future on a huge screen, we were all sitting there imagining what it would be like on the other side of the big transformation. An elusive notion. Machines had to become smarter and people had to become machines. Or the other way around. Led by the future prophet to a world without pain but full of intelligence.

It worked, that intelligence. Now they're eradicating pain.

Don't I want to remember or can't I remember? Everything is energy and information. Small particles. Energy can be generated, information gathered or erased. That's why the connections in our heads look like the connections in the universe. Maybe we're just a thought of someone we don't know. Maybe we're just a thought of ourselves. Who knows?

Here on my island, no two days seem the same. It can't be because basically my island is virtual. At least that's what it used to be called. I don't know why people clung so tightly to truth and reality of the life they had back then. And why that life wasn't virtual. When someone touched you, it took your brain a while to process what was going on, didn't it? That's no different now. And just before the big transformation, didn't they sit endlessly looking at screens? Didn't they call? Didn't they read books? Or did all those people who clung to their own biological bodies in such a way that only the things they understood were 'real'? I don't blame them. At least they could still die. Until intelligence took over. Maybe the old god was better than the new one. Who knows?

I had a very interesting conversation with an old ghost. He was sitting on a rock while I was dozing in my hammock. It was at dusk. "You know," said the old ghost who only wanted to be known as a 'master', "maybe it doesn't make any sense, but you can still do your best to believe in it? Can't you?"

"What's the point?" was my reply, "If it doesn't make any sense, why would you believe in it? What is, is and what isn't, isn't." "It would make your life a lot more bearable," said the master. According to the master, I wouldn't have to sit on this island (which actually wasn't an island but an institution). The sea wouldn't contain a mirror. That 'I' who would experience ebb and flow in the opposite direction would be just as ready as I am.

A witty thought occurred to me. The master would have to be very old or a very newly conceived program to still involve everyone in creation.

The 'new world,' as this creation is called, is a kind of continuation of the old with this difference: everything that can be experienced as unpleasant does not exist. Intelligence claims that man no longer has to believe in life after death. It exists. And it's even better than the versions that people had ever come up with. Intelligence has done it. This has to be said and, in a certain way, also admitted.

So far, my realities have been stronger.

The intelligence is kidding.

Pain is the expression of joy, because without joy you wouldn't know what pain was and vice versa.

I'm lying next to Marwan. He's stayed and together we do things. Like going to parties where we get drunk. Like wandering around town looking for breakfast. Like sitting at home with our laptops and entertaining each other with nonsensical actions. We've created our own bubble and no one's gonna crack it. Neither did Olga. Olga is now pregnant with Victor. They're married. I refused to be a witness. She didn't really understand. She married on a boat. Victor made her have to. Everyone was there, including Olga's divorced parents from Norway. It went well. There were golden flags. Afterwards, Marwan and I continued getting drunk in the bar I hadn't been to in months. In the basement was a sex shack. You don't want to know what's going on there. Marwan wanted a threesome, but fortunately we were too drunk and nothing came of it. That was yesterday. Today we take it easy. Marwan's making coffee. There's a gray haze over the city. The Rijksmuseum stands like an unwieldy dragon with its back to heaven. The Rembrandt Tower has its flashing lights on.

"That Victor," says Marwan, "that's a peculiar person." "Why?" I don't look up from my screen, today they found a solution for stem cells. "No one really knows where he comes from and no one really knows what his intentions are." "What kind of intentions could he have?"

Marwan stands in the doorway only in his shorts. We like a tropical climate. "We could get married, too." I stop reading. "Are you asking me to marry you?" "No, marriage is for pussies," Marwan says. And that's just the way it is. "I'ld like to cum." I don't think that's a problem.

I think what's going on between me and Marwan is hard to explain. Sometimes I doubt we're two different individuals. That's how easy and quiet our lives are.

Without an identity, effective action is impossible. Especially from a basement. So my first concern was to push new identities into the system unnoticed.

Every three days the scouts passed the endless numbers. An anomaly would be noticed. Process in four stages. Somewhere someone had to die and before this death was processed we had to intercept and duplicate this person. Processing someone's death, removing an identity, took as little as ten minutes so fast work was required. For the second phase, we had to wait for the scouts. Once they had visited and discovered nothing, we could proceed with the duplicate. The name had to be changed and the history. The name change was necessary to avoid confusion, but should not differ too far from the original. Anagrams. Other than that, it was a fill-in-the-blanks exercise. The iris scans had to be replaced, as did the voice recognition. This wasn't too difficult. Everything else could be modified to whoever we thought would be useful up there. Then the scouts came around again and we could reserve a chip. It was the year of replacement. A year and a half according to the brochure.

Getting on the reservation list was the last step towards citizenship. We made it all in the fifth and sixth week. At each birth we raised a glass of pinot noir, of which there were still a few bottles in the basement.

We had to get used to our new identity. Me

most of all. I had always seen myself as a man without one, so actually it was a relief when the deed was added to the thought. Identities are like charred bad breath I always thought, but somehow my new identity felt exciting. Like I was born again with unlimited possibilities to fool my head.

Because Marwan had registered in Berlin he had to pick up his reserved chip from his mailbox within thirty days. Victor's chip was delivered in Paris and Olga had to go to Milan.

I myself had to reach Amsterdam, partly by coach, partly by boat, partly on foot, and I had calculated that this would cost me about five nights. Which was actually quite fast, considering the detour I would have to make via Copenhagen.

Although we all only knew Victor for a short time, he inadvertently overwhelmed us with his knowledge. He spoke ten languages, including three program, fluently. Even Marwan, who pretended to be able to hack things, was impressed. Victor's life must have been boring and disciplined. He didn't talk much about it.

"Do we know the escape protocol?" Olga pronounces the words explicitly. Something's going on. Hour U is still ten hours away but already the elevator's coming down. No time to lose. Wake Victor up in the hammock, Marwan begins to pack the laptops, Olga and I retrieve the emergency equipment from the bags piled in a corner behind the hammocks. Now it comes down to diligence. Victor wriggles into his suit. Not getting noticed is the most important thing on our way out of this basement. The protocol must work. There's the elevator. In the elevator lies Viza's friend. Bleeding from the neck. We have to leave now.

Putting the tie into a pocket, I see Olga shove her heels into a handbag. The house no doubt surrounded and screened. Twenty-two hours local time.

I pull the keys to the boathouse off the wall and check my equipment before making eye contact with the others. Concentration. Earplugs in. Glasses on. Basically three escape routes. The elevator, the tunnel to the neighbors and the hatch to the garden. But these escape routes are also listed on the building sheets of the house in the database. The military police are surely waiting for us at each exit. Marwan is ready with the flares at the tunnel. Waiting for Olga's signal to fire. I press the second floor button in the elevator and step out, carefully circling the blood of our savior so far. The elevator leaves, we hope the plan works and the soldiers get in.

Olga, meanwhile, has her cell phone ready to ignite the explosives in the hatch. Victor and I are already standing in the recess behind the elevator shaft. As the elevator starts moving down again (we hear three men sneaking into it), Olga gives the signal. Marwan fires three shots into the tunnel. Three short flashes. Olga joins and Marwan manages to get into the recess just under the elevator as well, and then the fireworks begin. Knead bombs in the hatch, a tank of gasoline under the neighbor's house and the elevator covering our recess just in time. Hopefully the havoc we cause is enough of a distraction. The house shakes to its foundations. And then there is silence. The waiting has begun.

When I finally dare to look at my watch, it's three o'clock. The rescue workers must have been busy for some time. To scrape the burned remains of young men from the elevator. To pull out the twisted bodies of brave fellows from under the rubble of the neighbor's collapsed house. To pick pieces of flesh from the pear tree.

The boy is on his way down. Only now do you notice him. How did you not see him before? Walks past the cigarette machine. The muted light hits his face. At the railing you can see him all the way. Firm legs. A shiny green jogging shirt. Hard angular muscles in a loose hanging white halter shirt. Black stubby hair. Two cheeky little ears. For a moment, nothing. A brief flicker in the black holes where his eyes should be. Then the boy shuffles loosely down the stairs. Every movement of the boy strikes you as a slight tremor in your lower abdomen. Or in something that should have been your underbelly. 'Don't leave, don't leave,' you whisper.

The boy stays. Better yet, he briefly clings to a pole and turns with the pole in your direction. Begins a walk that lasts forever. Strolling. Slow sex motion. Along. If you weren't lying on the ground, bouncing against the walls, hanging from the ceiling... There you are. Like. Nailed to the ground. The boy walks by. Looks right through you. Slides down the stairs. Gone.

Raul had been sitting at home at the computer all evening. Finally he had managed to get a date who didn't live too far away from him. A hot one. Too hot. Jumped on his bike.

Ten minutes later pressed a bell. The pretty dude answered. Prettier than in the pictures. Raul had gotten nervous. Too beautiful. But you never know. Three minutes later Raul was on his back with the pretty guy inside him. The pretty dude turned out to be an idiot. Was aggressive. As if he wanted to thrust all his frustrations into Raul with his hard cock. It had not aroused Raul and when the idiot came growling, Raul was happy to put his clothes back on.

On the way home, light fog swirled in loose patches above the road surface. The chain on his bicycle rattled. Just a little. The sound lingered. Just as sounds underwater sounded more intense, displaced. In a square, under a pair of sturdy lanterns, a store window fogged half inside. A man with dark curls smiled dubiously from an immense photograph, while towers of the same book were stacked around it.

"How wondrous," Raul thought, "all I want

is a body to warm myself to, but then, when I find a body that I can lie against, I feel lonely and cold as if that other person only confirms what I already knew: that life only makes sense if you can live with yourself." Raul decided not to go home yet. To have a drink in town anyway.

After spending some time on the mezzanine, in a very sparsely lit corner on a wooden bench under which empty crates were stacked, perhaps it was time to take a look downstairs. At the very bottom of the basement were two rooms with even less light compared to the rest of the bar. Raul drank the last sip of vodka from his glass and let the ice cubes, which hadn't quite melted yet, slide around. Carefully he put his sneakers on the wooden floor. Out of the speakers sounded a clear female voice pledging her love to a stranger on a dusty beat. For a moment Raul thought of Olga who was also always in love with unknown men with whom she always had to go to secret concerts. Although Olga had never invited Raul to go with her to those mysterious gatherings, Olga had extensively warned him about places like these.

According to her, ghosts of deceased men wandered around such spaces, swallowed by the night, looking for a host. These spirits, unhappy souls, disembodied beings, sat in dark corners, waiting for a chance to cross over to something warm. Something with a beating heart. Something that breathed. These creatures waited just until they got their chance. That chance was limited to a single small moment. The moment of total release. The moment when the human soul briefly detaches from its flesh.

When Olga shared this information with him, he had looked at her pityingly, but she seemed serious.

Maybe she was jealous that she never got beyond the front door and that what happened behind that door was something she would never get a handle on. Maybe it was true and those creatures really existed and took over your body to do God knows what with it. Raul wasn't sure what to make of this thought. If good and evil existed, could it be that he didn't belong anywhere?

Raul walked to the railing where he had a clear view of the bar. Past the cigarette machine. The bar was not very full. The bartender was trying to flirt with a man who stared expectantly at the ship's ropes hanging in indefinable bunches above his head. A group of men stood sturdily with their bottles of beer in one hand and their other hand in their pockets messily scattered along the way down. Raul noticed, as he scurried down the stairs, how, one by one, the burly men turned their heads toward him and looked at him. Judging him. Attributing qualities to him that he might never be able to live up to.

For a moment he lingered on a pole. Deliberated with himself. Should he? Make the passage to the basement? Did it matter? The evening was lost now anyway. Raul turned with the pole on his way to the redeeming darkness. At the same time, he tried to hide his uncertainty and casually glanced past the men who were guiding him with piercing glances toward the basement stairs.

Downstairs, it takes Raul a while to get used to the darkness. In black tones of gray, he sees the entrance to one of the rooms. Raul strolls along the doorframe of what could be the gateway to a world driven by only one thought: the desire to be briefly detached from everything, especially himself. For a moment, Raul feels a hand slide along his ass. On the ground in front of him he discerns a pair of burly men squatting. In the last ray of light, which shimmers up from the floor to the minimum low turned, Raul sees hunks of wet naked flesh and a nipple ring. A smell of sweaty feet clamps down on his mind and, realizing this is happening with his tacit consent, he feels his pants being pulled down and his cock being devoured by a warm, moist cavity.

Raul is dizzy. How his cock is handled. Calmly. Patiently. Loving. Raul gives in a little. Punches his cock into the head of the man sitting there on his knees in front of him. This man knows what he's doing. Raul lets himself get carried away. Hungry, the man hangs onto his cock. Gives in with every thrust Raul performs slowly. It's as if this man's mouth was made for his cock. He fits exactly.

Raul braces himself. Tense his muscles. His hips the oldest rhythm in the world. Slowly mirrors the contracting haze in his head that increases in mass and begins to spin around itself. For a moment, everything stands still. Without a mirror. Airless. Lingers. And then. Breaks his skull. In two. In half. Cool, all-blinding light streams in, makes its way through his brain, bounces against every corner of his head, flows down his neck, past his spine to his tailbone. At his heart, the light coalesces, gets hot, shifts down a length, flows into his pelvis, and with the power and precision of a laser beam, it pops out through his cock.

For a moment nothing exists, but Raul completely falls apart. For a moment he is completely gone. If you look closely, you can see him vibrating out of his body in all colors. As if he seems doubly drunk. As if heat asphalt is melting. As if the pixels on your screen are asynchronous. Don't waste time now.

The kneeling man must have felt everything. Made the complete bundle of energy hit his palate. Admitted it dazedly. Caught it with his tongue. Made every thought melt. Petrified, the man remained in kneeling position while your hand rubbed along his ear.

"Thanks," he hears you whisper. You pull up your pants. Walk up the stairs. Wonder which coat is yours. Hand a crumpled pink piece of paper to the man shivering next to a radiant heater who manages the wardrobe. A green army jacket. You put it on. The coat fits like a glove. There are a few keys in your pocket. By feel, you walk to a bike and unhook it. You fill your lungs with thin night air. Look up. To the black sky where, far above your head, thousands of stars twinkle. Finally. You hope you don't live too far away.

As soon as I entered Raul, I had to synchronize. Fortunately, most knowledge is automatic. So I cycled with ease through Vondelpark to the student apartment that would become my home. I had never lived this high before and also found it rather miraculous that I had to take my bike into the elevator. In the elevator I had my first confrontation with myself. Amazed, I stared into my own eyes. I looked good. Beautiful. Exactly as I had wished myself to be.

On the way, I had already cursorily reviewed my memory. Few remarkable things came to mind, except that one face kept recurring. A smiling face that made me very happy. No doubt I would find out why.

Fortunately, I don't appear to have any flat-mates. The apartment is small and cluttered. A large map of Amsterdam hangs immediately opposite the door upon entering. It smells peculiar, as if a carton of milk has been sitting open for more than a week. I appear to own many books and papers. The cramped living room is filled with stacks. I didn't know I read. There is also a desk, a sofa bed and some boxes. From the ceiling hangs a lonely, pitiful light bulb. The view of the city is phenomenal. The window just about the entire length and width of the wall. The sky over Amsterdam. Low-hanging clouds catch the light of the city.

The wall to the left of the window is full of a single photograph. That smiling face that keeps popping up in my head. A beautiful man I see now. I remember copying the picture endlessly in a hallway with fluorescent light and thirty doors. But why?

There's dishes in the kitchen for about a month. I open the fridge, see it's empty and close it again. First a shower.

I don't wear socks and underpants. Just sneakers, a green jogging and a shirt. The mirror above the sink shows me that my face is almost regular. Black short curls, a pouting lip that easily forms a radiant smile. Regular healthy teeth, a firm chin with dense beard growth. Maybe I'll let my mustache grow.

I like my nose best. It has a blunt tip, is straight, not too far forward and certainly not too short or too long. Exactly right. It goes straight into my forehead without hesitation.

I have a thing for noses. A nose makes your face. That's just the way it is.

My eyes are big and green. A kind of sallow green. Eyelids full of pitch-black eyelashes. It's possible to look both dangerous and piercing and loving at the same time. I don't believe my own eyes! My eyebrows are wide and will grow together in a few years. They point on either side of my head to the middle of my ears. My ears are small, round and fleetingly bricked to my jaw. They hear well. Outside, an airplane sets off for landing.

I open the shower and let the jet get hot. Finally, a body again. And a nice body at that. I kick off my sneakers, throw the shirt in a corner and push down my jogging. Not bad what's hanging there. I'm very hairy but also very muscular. A good dark color. Big feet and firm calves. With the soap I go along all my new body parts to feel how soft and strong I am.

I know that in about a week I will be used to my new look so today I better marvel at my tight belly, hard thighs and hairy chest. No stress. Just getting used to it.

The shower spray isn't very strong. It pisses a little. But I don't care. I let the water flow down my neck and suddenly I think it's Saturday morning. What would I normally do on weekends? Maybe I shouldn't worry about it. The program must still be in my head somewhere. My dick's starting to pounce. It needs attention. I'm lovingly helping it to orgasm. I haven't felt this in years. Dazed I look at my own cum as it slowly drips off the white tiles between the drops of water.

I grab a sallow blue towel from the shelf above the door. No soft woolen treatment for my body, spartanly I scrub myself dry. With the towel tied around my waist, I walk to the living room. I sit down on the sofa bed and look outside. The clouds threaten a little through the lights below. In the distance, a plume of smoke rises from a tall chimney. Who is that smiling mister on my wall, anyway?

I am awakened by the phone. For the first time, I hear my voice clearly. "Yes?" A low frequency with a husky sound. "Hey brother, where are you?" It's Olga, I know immediately. We had agreed today to at least do coffee. "Where are you?" I ask hesitantly. "Oh, you're not alone?" asks Olga incisively.

"Of course I'm alone," I reply, "are you already at Renzo's?" (Did we meet at Renzo's? Where are they?) "No, not yet. Listen, I met a very nice man on the train. We're about to have some dinner. And I thought since we were actually supposed to meet up today..." (Well, thank god, not yet. I need to get used to myself first, let alone my friends.) "Is totally fine," I hear myself say. "Really doesn't bother you?" "Of course not, I was home late last night too, I think I'll stay in bed for a bit today." "How come? You sick?" "Not sick, just a little melancholic." I hope I don't sound too tragic. "It's really time you got over Marwan, we'll talk about it later. So you'll be home today?" "Probably, but don't pin me down on it." "I won't stop by. What are your plans tomorrow?" "Sounds like a plan," I say muffled, "give my regards to..." "Victor, his name is Victor. Maybe I'll introduce him to you soon." "No doubt." Olga never keeps men for more than a month, maybe two. Then she's usually done with them. Or them with her. Strange thought. We hang up.

Today I'm first going to explore the neighborhood. I can hear the neighbors arguing through the cardboard wall. So I don't really live here alone. And Marwan, is that the smiling man on the cardboard wall? Black and white times fifty. Marwan's laughing. Am I a masochist? Randomly I grab a pile of paper.

'Dass Raum und Zeit nur Formen der sinnlichen Anschauung, also nur Bedingungen der Existenz der Dinge als Erscheinungen sind.'

So I read German. Maybe it would be useful to go through all the piles today and see what I'm dealing with. Let's make some coffee first.

I wish I were a kite. With both my hands in my pockets, I walk against the wind. A rope attached to my chest would be enough to lift me up and drag me into the clouds. I think. I imagine what it would be like to suddenly be suspended above the park with a slight tug and to see the world from above, rocking lightly on the wind. Free, except for a thread, I would have an overview. At least of this part of the world. That would already be a great deal. Then, if I wanted to, I could steer myself with a single movement and skim right past the tops of the trees and then shoot up again, cheering, to a point from which I could launch my next attack.

"Hey Raul!" (That's me being called, I turn around.) It's Marwan. "Hi Marwan," I say as if I was expecting him, "what's up?" Marwan is wearing a green rain jacket and his dark blond hair is windswept on his head. "Good to see you. Coincidentally," Marwan laughs, "I was just thinking about you." (Marwan was thinking about me. Why, really?) My heart begins to pound. "Where are you headed?" asks Marwan. "Home," I say stuntedly, "I just had lunch with Olga." "Olga, how is she?"

"She's in love with an ex-Marine." "Good, I was getting a little paranoid about her. Can I walk with you for a bit?" As if he didn't already. Nikes.

"Where do you live anyway?" "In a student flat" "Cool. Do you know what I'd like most?" If I know what Marwan would want most. I have no idea, but I do know what I'd like most. I'd like to stop shivering and sweating. And I want my heart to stop pounding and I want to be able to keep my mouth and just talk to Marwan normally. "I'd prefer to live on the top floor of a flat with a view of the whole city. Marwan must be joking. "That's lucky," I hear myself say, "I live on the fifteenth. I just don't have anything in the house.

It's a wonderful feeling that out of nowhere Marwan has shown up. He makes some jokes about his weekend, but I sense he's looking for conversation.

Loneliness creeps up on you when you least expect it. Marwan's a hunk of a guy. As big as me and probably as strong. We must look like brothers as we walk along the gravel path chatting.

"A psychiatrist I used to see told me the question wasn't how to get a man, but how to get rid of him. I don't know if it's true."

As if truth still matters in this setting. After the transition, I'm not sure of anything any-more.

Marwan exits the coffee shop. "I've just opted for some Silver Haze. I hope you're okay with that?" Actually, I don't smoke. At least not those 'mind-altering grasses' that are farmed up in back rooms under daylights. Too much. Too loud. Too single-minded I am.

"I have no clue," I pretend. Marwan puts his arm fraternally around me. "We have to live a little, don't we? Don't we?" he asks mischievously. He's wrapping me up, but I'm already wearing the bow. "Absolutely," I agree, smiling shyly.

When we exit the elevator and I put my key in the door, I suddenly remember that Marwan is hanging on my wall in large numbers. How could I forget? I seem to be suffering from amnesia. Chucky-chucky-chucky-chuck. How would he react if he finds out I copied him and am using him as wallpaper? Is this even a wise plan? All I want is be with him. No, I want more. I want to be him. Or at least be close to him. Like right now. I'm sure he can handle it. It must be a shift of perspective. I think that's obvious. I dream too much of Marwan and now I will be found out.

(The digital version of my brain is one big gray hole.)

"So this is where you live? Super." Marwan walks into the kitchen and puts the shopping bag on the table. He sits down on the shaky folding chair that stands between the window and the fridge and looks thoughtfully at a spice rack that was already there before I came to live here. Suddenly my flat has a completely different interpretation. The light feels different with Marwan in it. The space is more spacious. It must be me. "I'll put that pizza in the oven," I say, "do you want a drink?" "I'll have a Coke," Marwan says absently as he's reaching for something in his inside pocket, "I'll prepare a joint. Do you have something to roll it on?" I give him a wooden cutting board.

"You know, I never used to understand why it was so important to want something. I never really wanted anything, but because it was considered normal to want something, I just went along with it." I didn't quite understand Marwan. "Do you mean nothing mattered to you?" "No, not like that, but looking at my own life, I see people expecting something from me all the time. No idea what exactly. And actually, I don't give a damn, but there's always this feeling stuck in my head that if I don't live up to expectations, I would be missing out. A fulfillment or destiny or just something for which there are no words. Something intangibly alive." "You have to explain this". I try to stand in as easy a pose as possible in the doorway, with my hands holding the doorframe above me.

"Hard to explain." Silence. Marwan slips his hand into the plastic bag from which he pulls out a tuft of weed. He grinds it finely between his fingers while he drops it piece by piece in the large paper. "It's a bit like what I'm doing right now. There was a party on Vondelstraat. I was taken by an uncle of mine, who does something at an advertising agency. A very fine uncle for sure. And I suppose he's doing an excellent job. In any case, he has an enormous house at the KNSM and flies every month to his apartment in Barcelona. His husband is there now. If I wanted to go to this party. A birthday of one of the associates or something, or one of his children. There were lots of balloons and lots of toddlers running around the house. When I walked in, a huge emptiness overtook me. There were a lot of people. All these people were doing something that I really didn't understand. A girl came up to me and started to tell me about her little business that she had just started. Something to do with web design or something. She pretended it was all very interesting and in between she told me who she had to talk to this afternoon and she wondered if she didn't know me from somewhere. All very confusing. I was introduced to a colleague of my uncle's who tried to have a 'conversation' with me with his tongue out of his mouth. But that failed because I didn't want to know why the latest slogan of a multinational was so bad. I mean. Those people over there, they're all working on something. They have an opinion and they need something. Want something. I don't understand any of that. What am I gonna do at a party like that?"

"Then why'd you go?" I looked into the oven meanwhile and saw the cheese was slowly melting. "Who knows? I assumed my uncle wanted to show me off. He introduced me everywhere with 'Marwan, the face of next year'," Marwan makes the quotation marks in the air with his fingers. "Like some kind of pimp." I didn't quite know what to say while looking at Marwan's face one more time.

Indeed extraordinarily beautiful, penetrating eyes, a sharp jawline and a strong nose with large flat nostrils. Pretty surreal to have 'next year's face' sitting on a wobbly fold-out chair in my kitchen. The joint was ready. Marwan lit it and blew hard at the glowing end once, sending sparks onto the black and white checkered tarp.

"I caught my uncle last week with some sad type. Now he's terrified that I'm going to tell Rogier that he's fucking other men". "Rogier?" "His husband. Do you want?" Marwan hands me the joint and I carefully take a hoist. Afraid I'm gonna choke or cough. "Rogier's been after me from the moment he's with my uncle. At their wedding, he still blew me on the toilet. I filled his mouth. I thought that was a fitting wedding present." Marwan now looks at me with a kind of loyal, confidential look. "Is the pizza almost ready?"

"Is that your living room?" Marwan walks straight to the door behind which I built my altar. From behind Marwan actually looks even more spectacular than from the front. Wide back, tight ass, firm thighs. Ears. "Yes, this is where I live," I report dazedly. I stay by the oven and watch the cheese begin to bubble on the pizza. I decide to take it out. In the front room Marwan is roaring with laughter. I hope I have chosen the right picture. "Are you okay?" I call out. I throw the pizza on the counter. Just a quick look anyway.

Marwan sits on my sofa bed and looks at the wall where he looks at himself laughing times fifty. "Some are not in line," he says. "I know, I'm not that mathematical". Exactly what I was afraid of doesn't happen. I myself would freak out if I came in somewhere and saw myself as wallpaper. Marwan doesn't. Marwan doesn't mind at all. "Still, it's not a bad picture," he says, as if he's talking about someone else. "You know, Raul," Marwan looks at me shyly, "I'm not the easiest." "I think that's obvious," I throw back. Marwan has to laugh. "Actually, and I know this sounds a little silly, but I'm honored to find myself here on the wall. You know me better than anyone. This is who I am. Perhaps there are even more of me. "

"We can always investigate," I suggest. Once I myself did not quite understand what or what for I should be able to catch light. It was as if reality was deceiving me. "How many do you think there are?" I ask casually. Marwan has a big smile on his face. "I like you," he says. "Give that joint another go? Then I'll cut the pizza."

After the sex, Marwan and I take a shower. He stays over and wakes up with me. Then we have sex again and skip the shower. He goes away and promises to call me. He never calls, of course.

I was mistaken. Marwan does call. Only a little later than expected. It's now five o'clock in the morning and I'm sitting in my underpants waiting for him. Intelligence is with me.

"But what are you going to do when Marwan's on your doorstep?" "How about letting him in?" "I see. Should I leave?" "Why should you? I don't do things I suspect I don't want to share with you, so stay if you like. Who knows, you might learn something!"

The intelligence evaporates. No doubt it won't be the last time I see him. The doorbell. I press the button from downstairs and hear the elevator moving up.

Sweaty, Marwan stands in my room. "I was suddenly reminded of you" "I've lost my way too," I reassure him, "Shall we fuck?"

Marwan is nervous. It's like something's going on. "You took me off your wall," he says. "Yeah, I got a little scared of you," I admit. The wall is white.

"Can we talk?" Marwan takes off all his clothes. "I'm on the run." "On the run? From whom?" I want to know. "I don't know. Do you have weed in the house?"

I still have that bag of Silver Haze from last time. I get up and snatch it from somewhere between my books. "I don't know where the papers are," I apologize. "Never mind," Marwan grabs his jeans and takes out a packet of tobacco. "Do you smoke tobacco?" "Yeah, sometimes." Marwan starts to roll a joint.

When he's done and I've made tea, Marwan starts talking. Remarkably calmer. He tells me he's found out he's not free. That he's tied to everything. That he can't as much as fart or it has an effect on others. "Are you sure you're not paranoid?" I ask cautiously. "If only it were true."

I wander off and think of the times I lost myself in eternity. How I floated above the park on a single wire. How I was surprised at every new twist of my destiny. Where did that time go?

She has spindly legs, a hollow back and a powerful jawline. Olga.

Olga's been swimming the wrong way in the twenty-five-meter pool for weeks. Nobody notices because at the time she swims, the pool usually is empty.

Olga is on a diet. Not because she's fat,

but because that's how it's supposed to be. Bravely, she swims her laps every day in this municipal pool.

Olga is wearing a dark blue bathing cap with white and light blue flowers. Just like the one she saw in Vogue. Within a day she had gotten her hands on it. A little store in the Jordaan. Her bathing suit matches her cap perfectly. Cut just below the waist, a very low back, spaghetti straps. Chocolate brown.

Olga is perfect. At least she likes to thinks so. She swims. Breaststroke. Her head just above the water. Nothing and nobody's stopping her. Her hour. Her break. Her fun. No one can take this away from her. With every stroke, the ghosts get smaller. Until they disappear into thin air. Then she can handle it again. The water wraps around her body like a cool, transparent velvet blanket. Carefully.

"Were you there?" The question is fired at her in plain language, unflinching.

Can she dodge it? Can she say anything but that? Technically she was there, if only she hadn't been so far gone.... Has she gone mad?

The king smiles mockingly from the wall behind her. The black leather handbag she had turned up at the Monday flea market is on the floor next to her. Her dress also black. Just some gloss on the lips and some mascara. No pearls, just the silver cross.

Okay. "Yes, I was there."

As if in a blur, the day in question passed Olga by. Was it true that Marwan lost it? Completely freaked out. Totally out of control. Dead? How possible?

The clouds pass laboriously over the park. There are people with dogs, people with children. Some bike, some jog and some have wheels on their feet. The first meeting. The last breath.

Sitting on a bench is Olga. Olga is an amazing woman. She writes me a card. 'Asshole' is written on it. I carry it with me all day. What happens between us. Marwan is mine.

One day, with a sun racing past the clouds, she sees him at the roses in the park. The roses, all still in bud. A few elders stumbling over the uneven red stones that hold the hexagonal flower beds together. And trees, almost green, swaying calmly, protecting this sanctuary. So excited about him who's approaching. Silence.

The moments before. She's sucking on a cigarette of an unknown brand. She's reading a book she doesn't remember. She's had a life that now could be called at best redundant. The moment itself does not last more than a second. Time is not linear.

Olga seems particularly relaxed, Marwan walks around in, what appears to be, just the kimono that falls open when he squats to pour the tea. "How do you like your tea?" he asks Olga. "Without is fine," she takes her cup, Marwan leaves the saucer on the table. He sits down next to the fireplace on a pillow. Black turns bluish-black, blue turns bright blue.

Marwan grabs a piece of wood with his right arm and pushes it into the fireplace. Now the light falls far into his kimono. Olga and I look breathlessly at his chest hair, which climbs in loose jitters up to his Adam's apple. "I am still a virgin," Marwan releases us from the silence that has fallen, "I still don't know whether to nail or be nailed".

I don't know what to think. I'm looking at Olga. She's still sitting on the couch with her knees raised. She's looking at Marwan, her mouth loosely open. Then at me. "What about you? You know what you like better?" The question slides into my head with razor-sharp precision.

"Help me with my zipper." She's turning around. Before I know it, Marwan is freeing Olga from her dress. He's naked. I can't believe it.

Salacious and fragile she sits there, her skin slippery satin, her forms twist in my eyes. Petrified, I continue to stare until the moment Marwan is inside her.

We're lying on the beach. Olga has a little car. We managed to avoid the traffic jams and find a quiet spot. The nude beach is always the least crowded, but you have to walk a long way to get to the first beach tent. I'm flying a kite. Marwan and Olga are lying half over each other. Marwan has a hard-on.

"Are we going to get ice cream?" Olga stands next to me. I look at her and try to avoid her breasts. "Good," I say. Marwan has walked into the sea. I haul in the kite and put on my shorts. Olga has a batik cloth tied around her hips. Yellow with orange flowers. Pale woman.

Silently we walk next to each other across the wet sand near the shoreline. Olga keeps looking over her shoulder into the sea as if she's afraid Marwan won't be able to swim. She should know better.

If she hadn't bumped into him on that drizzly Tuesday afternoon in that municipal pool we wouldn't have known each other. Maybe then nothing would have happened. Now we walked in silence in the burning sun to a wooden shack with flags hanging quietly, dead from their masts. I'll light the joint.

Marwan looks at me in the back seat through the make-up mirror in the sun visor. I pretend I don't see him and try to look past him as blankly as possible until he gives up and pushes the visor up with a languid gesture. Olga turns up the casbah lounge. To the sounds of a tormented woman's voice, we drive home.

I walk. Small steps. Cautiously. Dodging clutter. My foot bumps into something soft. Out of the corner of my eye. How the body of a woman in curious position blocks my path. Blood gushing from her neck. Eyes into nothingness. Dead deer. Mouth ajar. Tit out of her blouse. A big step. My left foot between her legs. Another step. Way clear to stage. Everyone is on their way. Olga resolutely beside me. Maybe it's just beginning. Twelve past ten. In front of the stage are three masked men with guns pointed at us. Another seven or so scattered around the room.

I remember the hostage action in Enschede last year. Lasted three weeks. Everyone raped by the hostage takers. Horrific history. For weeks a slow, white, silent march reigned on TV. Survivors. Trauma teams. Psychologists. Eyewitnesses. Experts by experience. Family members. Neighbors. The owner of the supermarket from around the corner. Lawyers. Lawsuits. Lynching. Bricks. Riots. Insurrection. Police force. Politicians. Distraught. Why. No why. Happens. Next to the man with the microphone is another man. Camouflage. Glitter curtain. Rifle slightly tilted to the floor. Disco ball. Masked faces go back and forth. Hard shadows. Could these be copy cats? Tough guys.

Someone taps his hand on a microphone. "We are here to rescue you," announces in nasal voice, "Please," clears throat, "can everyone stand up," loud beep, "Coming this way?" As the voice continues. Nothing going on. Everything under control. Go to sleep in peace. Calculate my chances. Use a napkin to wipe the Camembert off my hand. Try to estimate. How we are organized. Better cooperate. Nine past ten. I stand up. Lean on overturned table. Try to ignore havoc. Focus myself on man with microphone. Behind him two musicians on the floor. I recognize them by their suits.

The masked men are not just from the sky. They are everywhere. Some from the hallways. A few under the stage. Falling glass. Game shot

down. Frightened animals. Screaming. Shriek-
ing. I see myself diving to the floor. Crawling
to an overturned table with my hand in a
plate. The shooting stops.

Hanging from ropes, the intermission
number begins. They carry guns on their
backs, all five of them. Coming from the ceiling. Fluorescent light flashes on. Confusion.
The music stops. Everyone. Gawking at five
masked men. Camouflage descends. Silence.
Abseiling. Tssssh. Tssssh. This is not part of
the program. I'm not the only one who realizes
that. The shooting begins.

I brought a pen. Every now and then I place
a comment in the margin or scratch a thought
on a napkin. Maybe the two girls just ran away.
Had they completely had it with those morons
in the village or were being 'deflowered' daily
by 'an uncle' and were finally able to run away.
To flee. To escape from the mud where they
had been forced to grow up.

For a long time, I was not too sure of myself because I thought I was biased and because I thought I was taking every opportunity to escape myself, perhaps demonstrate that I could do just fine without myself. Now I am sitting by myself in a restaurant with a very high glass ceiling with palms and violins. Intimate. Distance. How it should be. Circumstances. I dragged myself here and forced myself to dine with a book so people won't think I'm pathetically sitting alone at a table. Awkward. Alone. Inside myself. Observing.

A truly free soul. Olga. Finally, antique Viking blood has yet to flow through her veins. While the middle is yet to come, Victor reaches for his beer. Perhaps Olga is more authentic than he can imagine. Two men in white and black rush to his table. Third course. Breaded camembert with elderberry compote.

Six past ten. At this point, Victor knows he missed the middle. He might have missed the middle. He looks again at Olga who is looking at the stage with big anxious eyes as in: 'Unbelievable how they are raping the music here.' Maybe not yet at the middle. Not all rules can be mastered. Not all rules bounded. What if time is linear? Or the universe is shrinking? Victor acknowledges a certain margin for error. He was always looking forward to a more adventurous life.

Olga slides. Across the table. Along the edge. To Victor. 'Beethoven-lite,' she giggles. The ninth symphony. Violins as a stringy chorus. Victor is overwhelmed; this is the third word out of her mouth tonight. Olga slides back again. In position. A glass of white wine. Pink voluptuous lips. Fickle. Victor lets himself lean back in his chair. His arms dangling alongside. He looks toward the stage. "Just a bunch of musicians in tuxedos."

Two tables away from Victor and Olga. I pretend to read a book. A fine book. According to the back cover. Brilliant. Gripping. Exciting. Moving. More than. On the front cover a picture of two girls walking into the fog. I'm sitting. For five days on page thirty-four. The girls have been murdered. Or kidnapped. In a basement. In the woods. They don't know yet. The whole village is looking. The inspector who will solve it is called Mazel. Puffy type. Whisky enthusiast. A birthmark in the shape of the Iberian peninsula. On his forehead. Translation from French.

So far so good. Reaching his goal. Victor is good. Getting better at it. The best. The middle is more than just math. Navigation, fact-gathering, intuition. Solution. Victor picks a piece of snot out of his nose and wipes it on the damask. No one sees it. Rules must be followed. Caution. Carefulness. Precision. Black shadows on the ceiling. Two past ten. Everything is possible. Overview. Insight. Disappearance.

Olga is in rose-red silk. It shines dangerously as it holds up her breasts. Victor takes a gulp of his beer. He takes in Olga somewhat more intensely. "She could be a supermodel," more raucously, "or a very expensive whore," more condescendingly, "Slut." His eyes slide along Olga's perfectly sculpted face. Gray-blue eyes. Blond bob. Brutal. Fragile. Her slender neck drills into her body like a knife. Victor sits ready. He knows. Somewhere in the middle he can escape. If only he manages to reach that point where he can pry himself loose. Free himself.

Situations have their own dynamics. One step at a time. Real space in real time. He looks at his cell phone. Ten o'clock. All he can do is wait for the solution to present itself. Always happens. Nothing without beginning, without end, without a middle. Victor feels them. Spinning like a solar system. That is going to blow itself up. Implosion. Fascinated by the middle. Black hole. Obsessed. Must. At all costs. Out in the middle.

Meanwhile, a small orchestra plays Beethoven on stage. People eat their five-course dinners while young men in white shirts and black pantaloons rush demurely through the room. Victor sits in a corner at a table under a palm tree. Together with Olga. Olga from Norway. From a fjord. A farm. That's about all Victor knows about Olga. Not that it matters. They've only just met.

The hospital room was white and quiet. A few times a day people in white suits came to look at me. I think plastic dripped through the IV.

When I was patched up, I turned out to be a man in his mid-thirties. What I was doing, I can't remember. Was I busy? Wasn't I ever busy? From the vast meadows of my youth with the freshly washed white sheets on the clothesline to the concrete and old bricks of a city that wanted to defy the past.

So I walked along a canal on my flip-flops. The sun, as usual, high in the sky. My head a hot air balloon floating along hundreds of feet above my torso. How the people around me, the trees on the waterfront, the houses on the street side, the boats in the water, the cars parked, turned into abstractions. Is there a way to still my mind, or is this just the way to break free from my instinctive self? Like I imagined wading through the mud as a child, looking for a way to free myself from my sluggish destiny. Not in the mud I wanted to be, but on the mud. Trick of the mind: in the cage, beside the cage, above the cage, behind the cage, on the cage, away with the cage. Managed to rise above the mud. To break free from all the turmoil of the world that, to my horror, held me back. Only rest could set me free.

Dreaming on my flip-flops along the canal. It must have looked funny. An old city with a middle-aged man in it who didn't know what to do with himself. Sitting in a self-built ivory tower. Bored, maybe even a little troubled by his own meticulously constructed world. A world only he could let collapse. If only he knew what the alternative was. But the alternative is never clear. Change we all do, but knowing where that change leads is a more complicated story.

Things you do for love.

Because in loneliness you drown.

CHAPTER 7

Everything is a quest. My mother was a woman alone. Abandoned by her great love, a sailor who came by once a year. I never knew him. My mother told me he had drowned in a storm.

She died when I was sixteen. Fell while she was cleaning out the closet in the bathroom.

She probably slipped, fallen awkwardly and broken her neck on the edge of the tub. A battle avoided is a battle won.

I buried her in the cemetery in the dunes. She had told me she wanted to lie there to be as close as possible to my father without leaving the country. My mother hated the sea.

The villa swells from the inside out and explodes. The fire comes out through the cracks in the wall which crumble and go up in smoke. Then he runs in the opposite direction into the residential area, where he is shot by snipers. We watch as his mighty body catches the bullets and spits them out on his back. Maybe it is wise to abort the mission, but now that we are alone, and in enemy territory, it might be better to take shelter and wait until we have an overview again.

We crawl into an old bus that is standing against a wall of crammed car wrecks and stay there. Silently waiting for what's to come.

But nothing comes. We suspect a trap. As if we are being watched by snipers or scouts, who must have been alerted by the ill-considered action.

Nothing. Nothing at all. The body remains in the middle of the street. Lost. Like pudding in a camouflage suit. The body should still be warm. The bleeding seems to have stopped, at least from this distance. Maybe our opponents don't have as much guts as we do. I'm thinking we'd better not gamble on that. I look at Marwan who is trying to overlook the cemetery through a few rusty holes. Tough guys. Time in slow motion. We've got to get out of here. Of the ten hours we've got for this mission, four have already passed. Headquarters are behind this residential area if our intel is correct.

I tap Marwan on his leg and he looks at me. I gesture with my head to the driver's seat. Marwan is frowning his eyebrows. I make a 'you never know' movement and together we sneak across the aisle of the bus to the front. Madness, of course. Just behind the driver's seat a wooden bulkhead has been built where we can hide. From this hiding place we not only have a view of the exit of the junkyard, a round gate with wrought iron fencing, but through the rear-view mirrors we can also see what's happening on the terrain, behind the bus. That doesn't look good. A group of men sneaks in between the car wrecks. Silently.

Our chances increase dramatically when we see the keys of the bus are still in the ignition. Who knows, we might get lucky and be able to go straight through the fence, past the houses with the sharpshooters, to headquarters in one go. It's a suicide mission. Basically, the mission has become that after that stupid action before.

I push the wooden bulkhead aside and slide into the driver's seat. Turn the key to ignition and give full throttle as soon as the engine starts. It does, as in a lurid miracle. Immediately bullets bounce off the dashboard in front of me. If we want to survive this, we have to give it all and be very lucky. In the rear view mirror I see Marwan hanging in the air between the luggage nets and using the open roof as if it were a foxhole. I have no idea, but later Marwan tells me that he has popped three men off the roof. That's how close they were. We speed along the lifeless body of our mate. I can feel the gunmen from the houses puncturing our tyres, but also on their rims this bus continues. We drive until we can't go any further. A barricade made of concrete blocks in the middle of the road is an obstacle we certainly can't cross with the bus. I decide to enter a house on the right. I shout "BANZAI" and with an enormous noise the front of the bus pushes into the front porch of the wooden terraced house that creaks and strangely enough doesn't stop the bus: we slide right through it. As if the bus has been given some kind of superpower, we're launched to come to a standstill behind the block in a vegetable garden. Marwan and I simultaneously jump through the doors on the right side that were open the whole ride and crawl under the bus to see from which side we can expect the most danger. We don't hear anything so we wriggle out on the other side of the bus. To make sure we get to a wall that rises half askew from the ground, ten meters away. As we run through the vegetable garden, the first bullets start to hit the ground around us. Yet we reach the wall just in time. In the firefight that follows Marwan and I take out about ten opponents. In order not to stay in one place for too long, I grab a hand grenade and pull out the pin. I count three, two, one, and aim the black egg in the direction of the other side where I suspect a few more shooters. At the moment the grenade explodes just in front of the balcony on the first floor Marwan and I are already a bit further, looking for new cover in this moronic hell.

Blink your eyes because in front of you is a house on which HQ has been painted in big letters. White latex on a red background. This can't be true. For a moment you don't trust your own observations and you think you're dreaming, but a bullet misses your ear and disappears into a head of lettuce further on. If this is the headquarters, as the facade indicates meters high, then you are crazy. Marwan scampers out in front of you. Each of you are on one side of the door, ready to go inside and ready to be shot. You don't know why the gunmen are missing. Not yet, The door's half-open and with your pulled AK 47, you're ready to shoot anyone who comes into your line of sight. Nobody.

You go from room to room. First downstairs, but there's nobody there, just some messy desks with antique computer screens on them. In one of the rooms, a fan patiently spins its rounds and quietly lifts up some paperwork. You start to move slower. Your breath is slowing down. Your pupils are getting big. In your ear you only hear the buzzing fan that keeps coming towards you. This house could very well be a trap. Too good to be true. You reach for the map in your breast pocket and fold it open while Marwan keeps an eye on the windows.

If this is headquarters, you can't believe it. What the hell are you doing here? There's no one here.

Then the ceiling creaks and like the devil's playing with it, the ceiling comes down. You can just jump to the side. The room fills with crackling noise and white dust. You're hoping Marwan's bypassed the dust cloud, too. With your rifle pointed at the center. What a havoc.

This is your fate: Not knowing what's going on and if you have a suspicion, always believe the opposite.

"Don't shoot, don't shoot," someone screams from the dust cloud while you are close to pull the trigger. "We're unarmed," hums a voice. As the dust cloud becomes more translucent you see three shadows on the ground. "Who are you?" you want to know. Marwan echoes after you. "Who are you? "Identify! That's how you know that he too managed to avoid the crashing group of people.

"Mission accomplished" calls one of the shadows, it turns out to be the old commander and two types of the secret service. Our corpse comes walking in and in front of the window are our former shot down opponents. "You passed with flying colors, boys. Welcome to the corps." You and Marwan get shoulder taps and congratulations and a bus with tinted glasses and air conditioning will drive in front of the building. A few hours later you and Marwan are cursing in the shower and after that there is a party banquet where all the important people also join in with strong stories about their 'missions'. The idiots.

Marwan and I decide it's fine halfway through dinner, walk outside and take the first Mercedes we see and drive it to the village further on. In the village there is a café with a dance floor and a pool table and lots of subdued lighting. We're the only visitors apart from two guests. The two men play darts in a corner of the café. When they are finished they come joining us. The bar lady, a huge woman with only three teeth, long dirty hair and greasy arms with failed tattoos, puts a bottle of vodka between us and announces she's going to sleep. The four of us sit together for a while, while the vodka slowly sinks into the bottle.

Life is simple. Floating through a sea of moments, moments where no fear or depression or joy or simply contentment is your friend. Where you go is unclear, where you come from is untraceable. The blank brain. Until you are confronted again with what is expected of you, what you expect of yourself. Dreams. Ideals. All those versions of yourself. As long as you know how to focus and control yourself, as long as you know what your goals, short and long term, are, there is nothing wrong. Nothing's going on. How long does a second last, how long an eternity?

The two men in the bar, Victor and John, are having fun and are challenging us to go for a ride with them. We say with some under-statement that we've got a car ourselves so if they want a lift we can give it to them. It doesn't seem like Victor and John are very keen on that now, but after a little insistence from Marwan, who appears to still have his service pistol with him, they seem to have less trouble with it. So we get into the Mercedes parked under the canopy at the back of the bar. Marwan and I in the front, Victor and John in the back seat. The child locks on the doors. While Marwan is playing with his gun a bit, I keep an eye on John and Victor through the mirror. They try to start a conversation but both Marwan and I don't talk much. After a while Victor, who seems the liveliest of the two, stops trying. By now we are driving on a highway through the desert.

I think it's a good idea to stop at a large

rock in the distance that lights up dark red in the moonlight.

I report "Sanitary stop!" and remove the child locks from the doors. Victor sees his chance, tumbles out of the car and starts running. I jump from behind the wheel and run after Victor in the dark. Unfortunately for Victor I soon overtake him and manage to hold him in a tight grip. Because of the adrenaline of the chase I got a hard on and only now I notice what a nice high butt Victor has. I pull down his pants and push my dick into him without hesitation. All on instinct. Poor Victor must be in too much shock to struggle against my violence. After I cum Victor starts calling me an asshole, dirty faggot and rapist.

I can't handle it. I'm gonna grab Victor's head and give it a firm twist. That's how I hold him while his body goes limp. I hate it a lot. Then all of a sudden I see that Victor's about the same size as me. If I really want a new future, then there's no better opportunity than right now. I try on Victor's clothes. It all fits perfectly. It's not easy to squeeze Victor into my uniform, but with a little stretching, breaking his right arm in the process, I manage. I'll find a driver's license and car keys in his pockets. I estimate the distance back to the village to be a firm walk. An hour or two. I drag Victor by his leg to the Mercedes where Marwan and John are waiting.

"Sorry," is my half-hearted explanation for dragging Victor along. I see fear in John's face. He's next and he knows it. Marwan commands John to take off his clothes.

We put Victor behind the wheel and tie John with his hands to the passenger seat. We put a heavy stone on the accelerator, start the engine and the Mercedes drives towards the motorway. On the other side of the road is a ravine and the surrounding area lights up because of the explosion.

You turn on the radio and the car fills up

with the complaining voice of a country singer who is dumped for the umpteenth time.

Not all rules can be mastered. Not all rules bounded. What if time is linear? Or the universe is shrinking? Victor acknowledges a certain margin for error. He was always looking forward to a more adventurous life.

"Let's catch the train," I suggest. "Good idea," says Marwan, and so we drive through the suburbs of the metropolis in the distance that chases its glass towers straight into icy clouds.

Wanting to keep everything under control is a form of uncertainty. It indicates that you don't trust others and because you can't count on them, you're insecure. You want to cover that uncertainty. You do this through control.

At the station, a rugby match ended on a screen. The news begins. Nothing about two soldiers having a car accident. The train is entering the platform. A commuter train running from the coast to the metropolis and now working on the last stations before reaching the business centre, and then the main station.

Opposite us sits a lady in a short, black coat with stylish blond hair and shiny high heels. With her ice-blue eyes she looks at me as if she has decided that I am a lion that needs to be tamed. A smile appears only on the left side of her mouth the moment she notices that I am intimidated by her staring. Outside, rain splashes against the window start to pounce and fan out my direction in small streams. I notice that by slumping I can almost touch the lady's shiny high heels with my feet.

I imagine these heels are so shiny that they act like a mirror and you can use them to see under her coat. I wonder what she is wearing under her coat. In any case, she wears inconspicuous flesh-colored tights with a little shimmer. A whiff of ladies' scent enters my nose and I look up. Right in her face. By now, her gaze has taken on something impersonal. As if I no longer interest her. Have I done something wrong? I try to look outside, the train begins to brake. As long as she doesn't get off. I need to say something, but don't know what. The train stops and she stays seated. When she gets off, I go after her. I need to know who she is.

Marwan is snoring next to me. I poke him in his side and pretend I didn't do anything. It's handy if he's awake when I'm off with the horny bitch. We've been through quite a lot these last few days. Maybe someday we'll run into each other again.

The train brakes and she gets up in advance. The moment the train stops, I shake hands with Marwan. "It was fun, goodbye." He doesn't seem to mind and just says "Good luck".

Just before the doors close again, I manage to jump out. There's another gentleman with a folding bike standing awkwardly in the way. Freak. I look around to see if she's still there. She's walking down the platform. She's got a transparent, plastic umbrella over her head. It's raining. I pull up my collar but it doesn't help. My whole shirt will be wet in a few minutes. I'm chasing my bitch. She puts her feet very sedate but decidedly on the ground all the time. Her ass seems to sway behind her just as her head seems to float under her umbrella. She hasn't seen me yet. Maybe she has a man sitting at home and is now on her way to him. Or is she not into men and that's why she looked so disdainful. I need to know. She turns the corner at the snack bar.

As I pass the snack bar I suddenly receive a firm thud to my chin. The blow is really quite unexpected and before I know it I am fighting with the lady from the train.

"Why are you chasing me?" She asks. "I find you horny," I answer honestly. I had never fought with a woman before and don't quite know what to do with her. Besides, she smells so good. I decide she can win from me, but when I surrender she stops hitting and kicking. "I like you," she says, "will you join me for dinner?" She holds out her hand. "Olga," she says. I introduce myself as Victor.

Finally the intelligence understands me. He sends Marwan over. I am in the back of the garden milking a cow when suddenly he is behind me. I smell him. He smells just as he did then. Hard to describe. We say nothing to each other. Calmly I squeeze milk from the udders. Firm jets into the bucket. I look ahead and see every hair of the cow soften, transparent. That's how moments like that go. You don't exist. Nothing exists.

"I've been thinking about you," I say, not expecting an answer. How many times over the past few years had I talked to him as if he were indeed behind me. How can I be sure he is behind me? "Are you still smoking?" I ask.

"No, I quit." Makes sense. What's the point of smoking if your whole life is one big orgasm.

THE END

About the author and the work

GJ Wielinga (b. 1971) began "serious writing" when he was thirty. First short stories and later novellas. All in Dutch, his second language, because he had never been taught to write in Frisian. "The most important thing about writing, is that you write," he tells anyone who wants to write themselves. For himself, writing a story is never really enough. To the question of a reader who asked if, according to Wielinga, a story could be without a plot, he answered in the affirmative. "Often life itself doesn't have a plot."

In addition to his work as a writer, Wielinga also creates visual art. "Experimenting from nothing to eventually creating a work that, through technique and choice of subject matter, nevertheless turns out to be part of a cultural tradition is the most wonderful thing that can happen to anyone."

This is also how The Digital Version Of My Brain Is A Big Gray Hole came about. It began with a number of short stories in which Wielinga wanted to see how far he could go with time definitions and perspective. Later, stories about friendship, sex and love were added. Wielinga left these stories until he returned from a singularity conference in San Francisco in 2007.

The future perspectives outlined at this conference intrigued him. If at some point people's brains will indeed be scanned and uploaded, where will they go? Do memories remain, or must they be re-arranged to fit the new reality? What is the value of emotions attached to these memories? Can humanity still feel if they enter a world where everything is perfect?

Wielinga pushed texts together, deleting and adding new parts, until the text tells the story of a man in quarantine on a digital island. Memories of a pre-transition life intertwine. It is hard to tell if those memories are real and if they are accurate. Perhaps it is just right that this man is quarantined. But perhaps it is also the shortcoming of a reality that is too malleable.

Publications by the same author

Short stories (Dutch)
2007 - Overleven in Deus Ex Machina
2007 - Het Is Maar Vlees in Bunker Hill

Novellas (Dutch)
2008 - Schaduwland
2009 - Het Beest Van Amsterdam
2010 - Het Wonderlijke Leven Van Mijn Zus
2014 - De Digitale Versie Van Mijn Brein Is Een Groot Grijs Gat

www.ingramcontent.com/pod-product-compliance
Lightning Source LLC
Chambersburg PA
CBHW031739150726
47989CB00006B/2531